WACKY!
Pets

By Teresa Domnauer

Carson-Dellosa
Publishing

SPECTRUM®

An imprint of Carson-Dellosa Publishing, LLC
P.O. Box 35665
Greensboro, NC 27425-5665

carsondellosa.com

Printed in the USA. All rights reserved.
ISBN 978-1-62399-140-1

01-002131120

Many people have pets. Some people have pets that look very different from most!

Afghan Hound

An Afghan hound
is a kind of dog.
It has a long nose
and long, silky hair.

Mini Hedgehog

A mini hedgehog
has pointy quills.
It can roll up
into a ball.

Rat

A rat is a smart
and clean animal.
A pet rat will sit
in its owner's hands.

Chinchilla

A chinchilla is
soft and furry.
It has big round
ears and eyes.

Gray Parrot

A gray parrot is
a large bird.
It can say words
just like a person!

Green Budgie

A green budgie
is a small parrot.
It can learn to sit
on a person's finger.

Potbellied Pig

A potbellied pig has
a big belly and short legs.
It eats a lot.

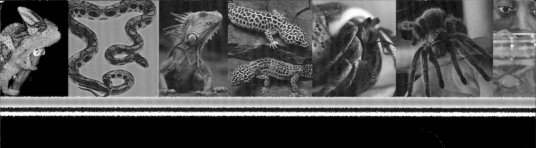

Chameleon

A chameleon is
a kind of lizard.
Its skin can
change color.

Boa Constrictor

A boa constrictor is
a big snake.
It can weigh up to
50 pounds!

Green Iguana

A green iguana is
a kind of lizard.
It has pointy scales
on its back.

Leopard Gecko

A leopard gecko has
dark spots.
It can live
for 30 years!

Hermit Crab

A hermit crab has
one big claw.
It finds a shell
and lives inside.

Tarantula

A tarantula is
a hairy spider.
It can be as big
as a hand!

Pet Care

All pets need care.
They need food, water,
and a place to live.
It is good to learn a lot
about a pet before you
bring it home!

WACKY! Pets
Comprehension Questions

1. Why do you think many people have pets?

2. Do you think a mini hedgehog would be a good pet? Why or why not?

3. What are two words that describe a rat?

4. How is a gray parrot like a person?

5. What is a green budgie?

6. Why do you think the potbellied pig was given its name?

7. How much does a boa constrictor weigh?

8. How is a leopard gecko similar to a leopard?

9. Which of these pets would you most like to have? Why?